NOV -- 2002

To my dear sister Kathy—in fond memory
of the golf club/tomato stake incident
—L. J.

eibboR dna rehpotsirhC oT —M. P.

Text copyright © 2002 by Lynne Jonell
Illustrations copyright © 2002 by Petra Mathers
All rights reserved. This book, or parts thereof, may not be reproduced in any form
without permission in writing from the publisher, G. P. Putnam's Sons, a division of
Penguin Putnam Books for Young Readers, 345 Hudson Street, New York, NY 10014.
G. P. Putnam's Sons, Reg. U.S. Pat. & Tm. Off. Published simultaneously in Canada.
Printed in Hong Kong by South China Printing Co. (1988) Ltd.
Designed by Gina DiMassi and Carolyn T. Fucile. Text set in Catchup.
Library of Congress Cataloging-in-Publication Data
Jonell, Lynne. When Mommy was mad / Lynne Jonell; illustrated by Petra Mathers.
p. cm. Summary: A young boy helps his mother realize how her bad mood
is affecting everyone in the family. (1. Anger—Fiction. 2. Mother and child—Fiction.)
I. Mathers, Petra, ill. II. Title. PZ7.J675 Wh 2002 (E)—dc21 00-068405
ISBN 0-399-23433-0
1 3 5 7 9 10 8 6 4 2
First Impression

When Mommy Was MAD

Written by Lynne Jonell

Illustrated by Petra Mathers

G.P. PUTNAM'S SONS ~ NEW YORK

Something was wrong with Mommy.
She burned the toast.
She banged the pots and pans.
And she forgot to kiss Daddy good-bye.

"Why is Mommy so noisy?" Robbie asked.

"I think she's mad," said Christopher.

Robbie was worried. "Is she mad at us?"

"Maybe," said Christopher.

"If we did something wrong."

Robbie looked at his shirt.

"I did my buttons wrong," he said.

"They wouldn't come out even."

Christopher fixed Robbie's buttons.

But Mommy was still noisy.

"Did you color on the walls again?" Christopher asked.
Robbie shook his head.
"No, but sometimes I color outside the lines."
"That wouldn't make her mad," said Christopher,
but Robbie wasn't so sure.

So he colored a new picture, very carefully.

He stayed inside all the lines.

And then he showed it to Mommy.

"That's nice," said Mommy—but she forgot to smile.

Robbie wanted her to smile.

But he did not know how to make it happen.

And he couldn't think what to do next.

"I must have done something *really* bad," said Robbie.

Christopher looked at Mommy.

"Maybe it's Daddy she's mad at.

Maybe it isn't us at all."

"It feels like us," Robbie said.

Christopher stood up. "Let's play inside.
Maybe when we come out, she will be happy again."
Robbie did not want to go inside.
He wanted a story. "Read about animals, Mommy?"
But Mommy wasn't listening.

Robbie wanted a snuggle.
But Mommy did not look very soft.
Mommy looked prickly. All over.

Now *Robbie* was mad.

If Mommy was prickly,

then he would be prickly, too.

He banged his blocks together.
He kicked his stuffed snake.

And then he bumped into Mommy.
"Bork," he said.

"What?" Mommy's hose splashed in her hand.
"What did you say?"
Robbie did not answer. He turned his back and
bumped Mommy over and over again.
"Bork," he said. "Bork. Bork. Bork."

"Robbie!" Mommy sounded cross.
"What are you doing?"
Robbie turned around.
"I am borking you, Mommy."

Mommy laughed a little bit.

It was a nice sound to hear.

"I can see you are borking me," she said.

"But I don't understand what you mean."

Robbie stood up very straight.
"I am a borkupine.
And I am borking you with my prickles."
Mommy looked at Robbie.
"You are a bork—oh, I see." She smiled.

Then she set down her hose.
"Are you an angry porcupine?"
"Yes," said Robbie. "Borkupines don't like
loud banging noises."
"They don't?" said Mommy.

"And borkupines don't like Mommies
who forget to kiss Daddies good-bye.
And they need stories and snuggles,
or they get very prickly."

"Hmm," said Mommy.
"I guess I'm feeling a little prickly, myself.
How do two prickly porcupines snuggle?"
"Well," said Robbie. "First you sniff noses to
make friends. Then you smooth down the prickles.

"And then you wrap up in something fuzzy
and be very soft together."
"What a good idea!" said Mommy.
"Can I be a porcupine, too?" asked Christopher.

They played porcupines all day.

And when Daddy came home looking prickly,
Mommy knew just what to do.

First she rubbed noses.

Then she smoothed down his prickles.

And then she gave him a big, soft hug.

"I'm sorry for borking you," she said.

"What?" said Daddy.

"Robbie will explain,"
said Mommy.